TOBY BELFER'S SEDER
A Passover Story Retold

Gloria Teles Pushker

TOBY BELFER'S SEDER
A Passover Story Retold

Illustrated by Judith Hierstein

PELICAN PUBLISHING COMPANY
Gretna 1994

*Special thanks to Rabbi Robert H. Loewy, Congregation Gates of Prayer,
Metairie, Louisiana*

---

*The word "Pelican" and the depiction of a pelican are
trademarks of Pelican Publishing Company, Inc., and are
registered in the U.S. Patent and Trademark Office.*

Library of Congress Cataloging-in-Publication Data

Pushker, Gloria Teles.
    Toby Belfer's Seder : a Passover story retold / Gloria Teles
Pushker ; illustrated by Judith Hierstein.
        p.   cm.
    Includes bibliographic references.
    Summary: Toby invites her best friend, Donna Barker, who is
Christian, and her family to the Belfers' Passover Seder, and the
Barkers learn about the origins and customs of this holiday.
    ISBN 0-88289-987-2
    1. Seder—Juvenile literature. 2. Passover—Juvenile literature.
[1. Seder. 2. Passover.] I. Hierstein, Judy, ill. II. Title.
BM695.P35P85 1994
296.4'37—dc20   93-5585
                                         CIP
                                         AC

Manufactured in Hong Kong

Published by Pelican Publishing Company, Inc.
1101 Monroe Street, Gretna, Louisiana 70053

The idea for this story was suggested by non-Jewish friends who wanted to know the meaning of Passover.

The Seder, a combination banquet and religious service, tells of the miraculous deliverance of the children of Israel from Egyptian bondage.

The Seder was a very important part of my childhood. We celebrated with beloved grandparents, parents, sisters, brothers, aunts, uncles, cousins by the dozens, and many, many friends.

With deepest love this book is dedicated to them all.

And to my three wonderful daughters for keeping this beautiful tradition alive.

And to Ben.

TOBY BELFER'S SEDER

Toby Belfer and Donna Barker were best friends. They lived next door to each other in a small South Louisiana town. They shared the same birthday and sat next to each other in school. Toby and Donna played tricks on each other as best friends often do. They did everything together except go to Sunday School. Toby was Jewish and went to Sunday School at the synagogue in the next town. Donna was Christian and went to the church Sunday School nearby.

It came as no surprise, then, when one spring day the Belfers invited the Barkers for Passover Seder.

"What shall I wear?" asked Donna.

"Anything you want," answered Toby.

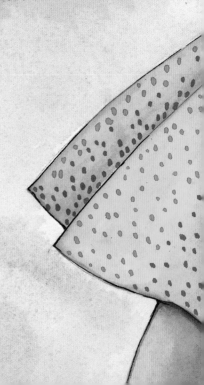

Toby's grandparents from the city soon arrived with their car full of goodies for the delicious Seder meal they were going to help prepare.

They even brought **Haggadot** with them. A Haggadah is a special book that tells the story of Passover with songs, rhymes, and symbols and gives the order of the Seder. Each person at the Seder has one to read.

Toby and Donna greeted Toby's grandparents with lots of hugs and kisses. As the girls helped with the packages, Donna said, "I've been invited for Seder, too. What shall I wear?"

"You can wear your Easter dress," replied Grandmother.

Everyone works hard getting ready for Passover—there is lots of cooking and spring-cleaning to be done.

Small pieces of bread are placed throughout the house and collected again. This is known as ridding the house of **hametz.**

"During Passover we don't eat bread or bread products. It should not even be in the house for the eight days of Passover," explained Toby.

Donna and Toby helped set the long table with beautiful china, crystal, and silverware used only at Passover time. They set an extra silver wine goblet out for the prophet Elijah. According to legend, Elijah is the messenger of peace who visits every home where Seder is held.

Everything on the Seder table has special meaning. A beautiful Seder platter is placed at the head of the table. On it is **karpas**, a sprig of fresh parsley to represent the green of springtime; **maror**, a little horseradish to remind us of the bitterness of slavery; **haroset**, a mixture of chopped apples, nuts, cinnamon, and a few drops of wine. This mixture represents the bricks that the slaves made to build the pyramids for the Egyptian Pharaoh.

Also on the Seder platter is the **pesach**, a roasted shank bone to remember the sacrifice of the Paschal lamb made in ancient days; and **baytzah**, a hard-boiled egg that represents the continuity of life.

Next to the Seder platter is a separate plate with three pieces of **matzah.** This is the unleavened bread Jewish people eat instead of regular bread during the Passover season. Each matzah is placed in the folds of a lovely napkin especially decorated with the symbols of Passover. Toby made hers in Sunday School.

Father will hide half of the middle matzah called **afikoman** for the children to find later.

For everyone, on smaller plates are some horseradish, haroset, parsley, egg, and matzah. There is also a small cup of salt water.

"We will dip the parsley, representing springtime, into the salt water and eat it to remember the tears shed by our ancestors when they were slaves in Egypt," explained Toby.

Now that the table was set, Toby walked Donna home to get dressed.

"But what shall I wear?" Donna asked, worried.

Without a hint or smile that she was only joking, Toby said, "My little cousins, who will recite the four questions, always wear white sheets."

Donna thought about it and decided that's what she wanted to wear, too.

When the Barkers arrived at the Belfers' house in time for Seder, Donna was dressed in her lovely pink Easter dress, but she was holding a fresh white, starched and ironed sheet. She said she hadn't known how to put it on herself, so she brought it folded.

Still without a hint that she was only joking, Toby wrapped the sheet over Donna's shoulder and around her like a toga, and what was left over, she draped over Donna's head.

Donna looked beautiful—just like someone from ancient days, but no one else was wearing a sheet!

Donna laughed and laughed when she realized that Toby had played a trick on her. Her little pink Easter dress was darling, and she was dressed in very good taste without the sheet.

When all the friends and relatives arrived from far and near, everyone was seated at the beautiful table. The Seder was about to begin.

Toby's Papa, as her grandpa was affectionately called, and her father sat at opposite ends of the table with a pillow behind their backs. This night they were allowed to lean on their elbows because in ancient days this was the position of free men.

Mrs. Belfer lit the holiday candles, held up her hands, and said a blessing,

"Baruch atah Adonai, Elohenu melech ha'olam asher kidishanu, bamitzvotav vitzevanu lahadlik ner shel Yom Tov. Amen.

"Blessed art Thou, O Lord our God, Ruler of the universe, who commanded us to kindle the lights of Passover. Amen."

Then they all lifted the first of four cups of wine. The children had grape juice. Mr. Belfer said,

"With song and story and the symbols of the Seder, let us renew the memory of our past.

"Baruch atah Adonai, Elohenu melech ha'olam bore pa-re hagafen.

"Blessed art thou, O Lord our God, Ruler of the universe, who created the fruit of the vine."

All drank the first cup of wine or grape juice. He also said,

"Baruch atah Adonai, Elohenu melech ha'olam shehecheyanu vekeyemanu vehigianu lazman hazeh.

"Blessed art Thou, O Lord our God, Ruler of the universe, who gave us life, sustained us, and brought us to this happy season."

Everyone read together, "For lo, the winter is past, the rain is over and gone, the flowers appear on the earth; the time of singing is come and the voice of the turtledove is heard in the land" (Song of Songs).

Papa then lifted the plate of matzah and said, "This is the bread of affliction eaten by our ancestors when they were slaves in Egypt. Let all who are hungry come and eat.

"Baruch atah Adonai, Elohenu melech ha'olam, asher kidishanu, bamitzvotav vitzevanu al achilat matzah.

"Blessed art Thou, O Lord our God, Ruler of the universe, who commanded us to eat unleavened bread."

Toby's little cousins asked the four questions. This is a special role for the youngest present. They had practiced a long time to get the Hebrew right.

"Mah nish-ta-nah ha lailah hazeh mikol ha-lei-lot?"

"Why is this night different from all other nights? On other nights we eat bread or matzah. Why on this night do we eat only matzah?

"On all other nights we eat any kind of herbs. Why on this night do we eat especially bitter herbs—like horseradish?

"On all other nights we do not eat haroset. Why on this night do we eat haroset and why do we dip greens in salt water?

"On all other nights we sit upright at the table. Why on this night may we lean?"

Then came the story of Passover and some answers to the questions.

More than 3,000 years ago the Jewish people lived in a land called Egypt. At that time, there ruled a cruel Pharaoh who made slaves of the Israelites, as the Jews were known. They worked from morning until night making bricks to build the pyramids.

Now, in Egypt lived an Israelite man named Moses. When Moses saw how badly the Jews were being treated, he felt great pity and wanted to help them.

Then God called Moses and his brother Aaron to Pharaoh to ask him to free the Israelites.

Pharaoh refused. Instead, he ordered his taskmasters to work them even harder.

Because Pharaoh would not obey, God sent ten plagues upon the Egyptian people and every Egyptian home suffered. These troubles **passed over** the homes of the Jews. That is why the Bible calls this holiday Passover.

Pharaoh became convinced after the tenth plague and he gave up at last.

When Pharaoh said that the slaves could go free to worship their God, they had to hurry and pack up as quickly as possible. They couldn't take very much with them. They put the dough for their bread on boards and carried them on their backs.

The hot sun baked the dough, and instead of rising as usual, the bread took on the shape of matzah.

So you see, Passover celebrates the escape from Egypt and our freedom from slavery. Had God not redeemed our fathers and mothers from Egypt, we, our children, and our children's children would have remained slaves.

Father said, "Now that we have talked about the pesach, the matzah, and the maror, let the feast begin."

The ceremonial Passover platter was removed and dinner was served.

After a scrumptious meal of fish, soup, roasted lamb, vegetables, and dessert, the children searched for the afikoman.

The one who finds it usually gets a prize, but Papa gave each child one to remember this wonderful Passover night.

Donna was the lucky one to find that little piece of matzah so she got two prizes. You should have heard the cheering!

"But wait, it's not over yet," said Toby. "We have to say grace."

Everyone was seated at the table again.

More prayers of thanksgiving were said. It is customary to linger over the Passover table singing hymns.

Riddles and rhymes were said especially for the children's enjoyment. At the end, everyone said, "Next year in Jerusalem."

Donna looked puzzled.

"Not really," said Toby. "That is just our way of wishing each other freedom and peace!"

THE PARALLELS BETWEEN
PASSOVER AND EASTER
ARE STRIKING

1. Both holidays are rooted in historical recollection.
2. Both festivals contain elements of the miraculous.
3. Both are festivals of redemption.
4. Both festivals emphasize freedom and give hope to man.
5. So it was, as some scholars have written, that Jesus and his disciples praised God at the Last Supper.

RABBI KENNETH I. SEGEL

DAYENU

Father asks, "How many wonders did the Eternal perform for us?"

Had God brought us out of Egypt, only brought us out of Egypt—DAYENU.

Had God split the sea before us, only split the sea before us—DAYENU.

Had God given us the Sabbath, only given us the Sabbath—DAYENU.

Had God given us the **Torah**, given us God's law to guide us—DAYENU.

Ilu hotsi, hotsianu, hotsianu, mi Mitsraim
  Hotsianu mi Mitsraim, Dayenu.

Ilu natan lanu, natan lanu, et ha Shabat, Dayenu.

Ilu natan lanu, natan lanu, et ha Torah, Dayenu.

Ilu hichnisanu l'Erets Yisrael, Dayenu.

לְשָׁנָה הַבָּאָה בִּירוּשָׁלָיִם.

GLOSSARY

AFIKOMAN—The Greek word for dessert. A piece of matzah is broken and hidden. This piece of matzah is the afikoman. The children search for it and return it before the end of the Seder. A reward is given to the one who finds it.

BAYTZAH—A hard-boiled egg to represent the continuity of life.

DAYENU—Hebrew for "It would have been enough."

KARPAS—Fresh parsley to represent the green of springtime.

MAROR—Horseradish to remind us of the bitterness of slavery.

MATZAH—Unleavened bread, which symbolizes the hasty flight the slaves made when they left Egypt. Wine symbolizes life.

PESACH—Roasted shank bone to represent the sacrifice of the Paschal lamb made in ancient days. Another name for the roasted shank bone is **zaroa**.

TORAH—The first five books of the Old Testament.

BIBLIOGRAPHY

Bernard, Rose, ed. *A Haggadah for Our Time*. Illustrated by Florence Sloat. Los Angeles: Bernard, 1962.

Central Conference of American Rabbis Staff. *A Passover Haggadah: The New Union Haggadah*. rev. ed. Edited by Herbert Bronstein. Illustrated by Leonard Baskin. New York: Central Conference of American Rabbis, 1982.

Levin, Meyer. *The Haggadah*. New York: Behrman House, 1968.

Mervis, Leonard J. *We Celebrate the Jewish Holidays*. New York: UAHC, 1952.

Rosten, Leo. *The Joys of Yiddish*. New York: McGraw-Hill, 1968.

Segel, Kenneth I, ed. "A Passover Guide." Pamphlet.